the search for
THE SMELL OF CHRISTMAS®

☆

the
search
for

THE
SMELL
OF
CHRISTMAS

By Richard Upton and Sharon Fair

Illustrations by
Bonnie Kay Buerkle

Copyright © 1992 by Richard Upton and Sharon Fair

Library of Congress Cataloging-in-Publication Data
92-081976
Upton, Richard and Fair, Sharon   The Search for the Smell of Christmas

Summary: One of Santa's elves goes in search
of the smell of Christmas.

ISBN 0-9633348-0-8

Published in Heber Springs, Arkansas

First Edition

Designers: Ronnie Stoots and Debby Weiss

Typography and Composition: The Towery Design Group

Color Separations and Printing: Lithograph Printing Company

To Miss June and Little Gator
R.H.U.

To Nicholas and Jacob
S.P.F.

To Christina
B.K.B.

Christmas was drawing near once again. Santa Claus sat with Mrs. Claus in their cozy, warm kitchen. Mrs. Claus was sticking cloves into oranges while Santa sipped hot chocolate with marshmallows. Everything was running smoothly at the toy factory and the elves were working very, very hard. But Santa was troubled because he had not been able to think of anything new and wonderful for Christmas. Time was running short... very short.

Santa rose from the table and paced back and forth, back and forth in front of the crackling fire thinking hard about discovering something new for Christmas.

"What is troubling you, Santa?" Asked Mrs. Claus.

"I want to find something new to give to the world for Christmas this year," replied Santa. "I have not had any new ideas for several years. I just do not want to disappoint the children."

"You're right," smiled Mrs. Claus, amused at Santa's grumbling. "Perhaps you should go and see Whiffle the elf. I hear rumors that he always has many good inventions in the works, but just cannot seem to finish anything. Maybe the two of you could help one another."

Santa set off for Whiffle's house with a frown on his face. He knew that Whiffle was a nice, hard working elf but he was just never able to finish anything because of his large, very large nose. Whenever he caught a "whiff" of anything that smelled good, Whiffle lost all concentration and went in search of the smell. That is how he got his name "Whiffle." Santa doubted that he could put his large, very large nose, to the grindstone long enough to find something new for Christmas.

In the meantime, Whiffle sat in the cellar of his little elf cottage working away on his latest invention. For years and years, Whiffle had labored away in his little cellar trying to invent something new for Christmas. He knew that all the other elves laughed at him because his large, very large nose, distracted him every time he had a good idea.

But this year was going to be different. Whiffle had gone to see Sage, the wise old elf, and asked him for his help. "Sage, the wise one," groaned Whiffle, "Everyone makes fun of me because I cannot finish anything I start. My large, very large nose, lures me away whenever it smells anything good. What am I going to do?"

"Whiffle, Whiffle, my nosey, little friend," chuckled Sage. "What distracts you attracts you. Put this nose of yours to good use and find something that will make the world a better place. After all, the nose knows!"

"My nose just gets me into trouble," grumbled Whiffle.

"You have a great nose," said Sage. "You must learn to make your nose work for you . . . just like your eyes and ears work for you. Find a way to use your nose wisely. If you do, it will lead you to great things . . . it could even make you famous!"

Whiffle thanked Old Sage for his advice, and trudged back through the snow to his cottage cellar.

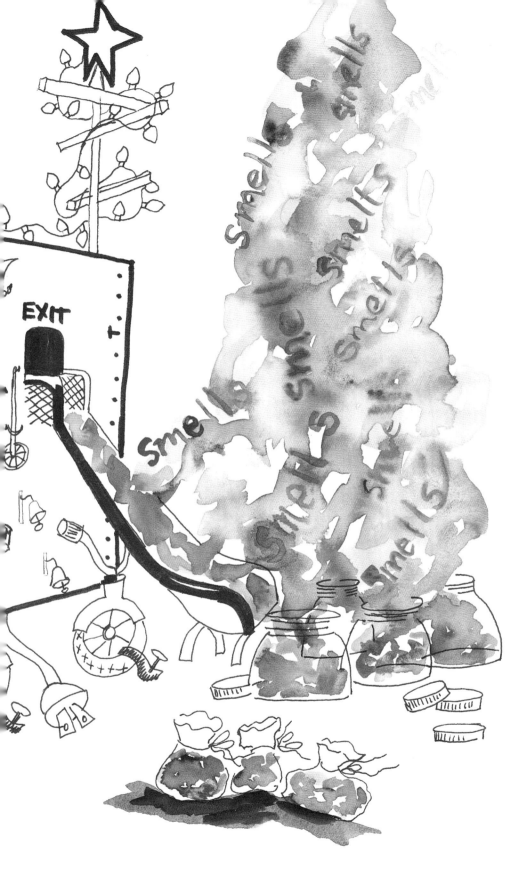

It was here that Santa found Whiffle, hard at work on his latest invention. He had taken Old Sage's advice and worked on something that interested his nose!

Whiffle was so very happy and pleased to see Santa.

"Ho, Ho, Ho, Whiffle," said Santa. "I have come to seek your help to find something new and wonderful for this Christmas. Do you have any new ideas or inventions that might help me?"

Whiffle could not believe his luck. He almost burst with excitement.

"Santa, Santa, I have just the thing," said Whiffle, jumping up and down. He showed Santa his new invention. "I call this my 'Smell Like' Machine," he boasted. "You draw a picture of the smell that you want and the machine will find that smell for you."

Whiffle drew a picture of an Apple and put it into the machine. The 'Smell Like' Machine began to shake and rattle and "WOOF" out came the wonderful smell of Apple. Santa was 'Nuts about Apples' and cheered Whiffle's invention. Encouraged by Santa's response, Whiffle drew another picture, this time it was a peach. He put it in the machine and, "WOOF" out came the sweet smell of a peach. Santa was very impressed.

"Good work, Whiffle! But, how can we use this invention to find something new and wonderful for Christmas?" Asked Santa. He and Whiffle paced back and forth, back and forth thinking hard about this problem. Suddenly, Santa threw his hands up and exclaimed,

"Whiffle, by jove, I have it! We will use your 'Smell Like' Machine to create the Smell of Christmas. This year we will give the Smell of Christmas to the entire world. What a wonderful idea!

"Oh yes, this is great," shouted Whiffle, and he grabbed his pad and crayon, then stopped short. "But Santa, how do you draw a picture of Christmas?"

Santa thought about this for a minute and replied,

"That is a very good question, Whiffle. I do not know. But Christmas is just a week away and we must find something that will make your machine give us the Smell of Christmas as soon as possible. I have to work on my list of good little girls and boys, so I must ask you to find the Smell of Christmas for me. Can you do it? Can you keep your nose pointed in the right direction?"

"I will certainly do my best, my very best, to find the Smell of Christmas for you Santa," said Whiffle.

With that Santa returned to the toy factory and Whiffle set out to find the Smell of Christmas.

W hiffle thought about what old Sage had said to him "What distracts you
attracts you… The Nose Knows… Make the world a better place…"
Whiffle knew what he had to do. He had to follow his nose.

So, he dashed to the train station and took the overnight elf express due
South. Each year at Christmas time he had always been distracted by a
smell in the air, but he never knew what made the smell or from where it
was coming. The only thing he knew for certain was that it was very strong
when the wind blew from the South.

So Whiffle sat on the elf express as it rambled over mountains and through valleys with his large, very large nose, poking out the window as he searched for the Smell of Christmas. Once he had the elf conductor stop the train as they approached a forest with giant snow covered pine trees. Whiffle took a big "whiff" of the air. It was the smell of the trees and he liked it very, very much. But it was not quite the smell that he remembered. "Keep going," he shouted, and stuck his large, very large nose, even further out the window as the elf express puffed and steamed through the falling snow.

As the train approached a small town nestled between two mountains, Whiffle got a big "whiff" of the most wonderful smell that his large, very large nose, had ever smelled.

"This is it! This is it! Stop the train," he shouted to the elf conductor.

Whiffle scurried out of the train, nose held high, and followed the smell to a small white house with a white picket fence. Snow covered the roof and smoke was coming from the chimney. The smell of cedar from the nearby forest rose into the air. He peeked into the window of the little house.

Inside he saw a beautiful green Christmas tree with brightly colored packages underneath. The fire was crackling in the fireplace and two stockings hung from the mantle. A bowl of warm roasted chestnuts sat on the hearth. In the kitchen cinnamon sticks were simmering on the stove and a freshly baked orange cake sat cooling on the cupboard. A huge turkey was in the oven and the stuffing was mixed up in a bowl. The table was set for dinner with red candles and holly decorating the center. Two children were in the den stringing popcorn for the Christmas tree, laughing merrily.

And the smell that was in the air! It was wonderful! It was...Magic! The Magical Smell that only Christmas can bring!

Whiffle scampered around the little house and gathered up pine cones, hickory nuts, sweet gum balls, red berries, and other greenery and put them in his pocket.

"I will draw pictures of all these things and put them in my 'Smell Like' Machine," thought Whiffle. "All mixed together they should be like this magical smell."

Whiffle hurried back to the elf express and ordered the elf conductor to rush back to the North Pole. Time was running short and Santa was counting on him.

Back in his little cottage cellar Whiffle feverishly drew pictures of pine cones, hickory nuts, sweet gum balls, red berries, cinnamon sticks, oranges, and all the other things he had seen and gathered from around that happy little house. He put them into the 'Smell Like' Machine. The Machine began to rattle and shake and "WOOF", out came...**NOTHING!**

"Oh, no!" Shouted Whiffle.

He could not believe it! It was terrible! It was awful! He was so disappointed.

"What could be wrong!" He cried.

What was he going to do now? He could not bear the thought of disappointing Santa and all the children. And, to make matters worse, he was sure all the other elves would laugh at him once again.

"Old Sage has just got to help me," thought Whiffle, and he rushed off to his cottage.

Old Sage calmed Whiffle down and patiently listened while he explained his problem. He told Sage how he had followed his advice and used his nose to find the Smell of Christmas.

"I was so certain that all these things mixed together would give me the smell that I found at the little white house in the mountains," cried Whiffle. "But when I put the pictures into the 'Smell Like' Machine, NOTHING HAPPENED. NOTHING!"

Sage smiled knowingly and said,

"Whiffle, Whiffle, my nosey friend, your nose HAS been your faithful friend. It led you in the right direction, did it not? But something is wrong with the way you tried to make the Smell of Christmas. Think hard now, Whiffle. What is it that made the smell so special?"

W hiffle closed his eyes very tight and thought about that little white house in the mountains. He thought about the warm feeling he got when he saw the happiness and love inside. The warm feeling of happy hearts. Laughter in the air. Joy in people's eyes. The Magic of Christmas.

It was then that Whiffle realized what was missing. This smell was more than a smell. It was a FEELING. That was the problem. His 'Smell Like' Machine was just that, a machine. It could not FEEL Christmas. Only people could do that.

At that moment, all around Whiffle there was a soft yellow glow shimmering with stars. Whiffle was surrounded as more and more star dust settled to the floor. The room in old Sage's cottage was filled with that magical smell that Whiffle had found around that little white house in the mountains. At that very moment, on that cold and wintry night, the Smell of Christmas was born in the heart of Whiffle the elf.

"Congratulations, Whiffle," smiled Old Sage. **"You have discovered the Magic that makes the Smell of Christmas."**

Old Sage gathered up the Magic star dust that had fallen all around Whiffle and put it in a small bag.

"This should be enough for this Christmas," said Old Sage as he handed the bag to Whiffle.

When Santa heard about the special way that Whiffle had discovered the Smell of Christmas he declared,

"the tale of Whiffle the elf and the search for the Smell of Christmas will be told many, many times for years to come. It will become a legend of the North Pole. Children will learn that the magic that makes the Smell of Christmas comes from the love in their hearts.

On Christmas Eve that year, Whiffle was given the honor of sitting next to Santa Claus in his sleigh. As the team of reindeer soared through the skies, Whiffle scattered the Magical Smell of Christmas all over the world. And just as Santa Claus had foretold only those who carry the Magic of Christmas in their hearts truly know, and will always remember, the Smell of Christmas.